# ELMO LOVES YOU

## A Poem By ELMO

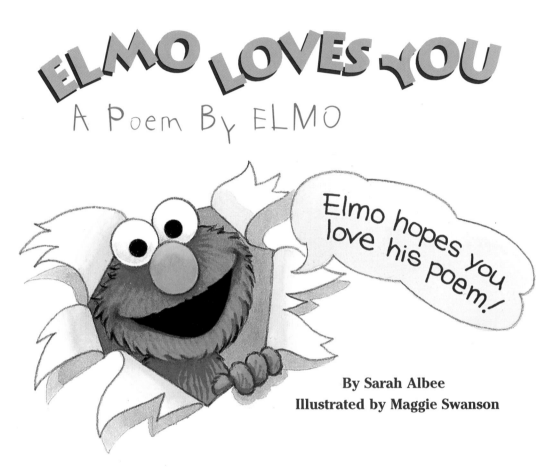

Elmo hopes you love his poem!

**By Sarah Albee**
**Illustrated by Maggie Swanson**

*Featuring Jim Henson's Sesame Street Muppets*

**A GOLDEN BOOK • NEW YORK**

Golden Books Publishing Company, Inc., New York, New York 10106

Published by Golden Books Publishing Company, Inc., in cooperation with Children's Television Workshop

A portion of the money you pay for this book goes to Children's Television Workshop.
It is put right back into SESAME STREET and other CTW educational projects. Thanks for helping!

Everyone loves something.
Babies love noise.
Birds love singing.

Kids love toys.

Bert loves pigeons, and pigeons love
to coo.
Can you guess who Elmo loves? Elmo
loves *you*!

Piggies love to roll in mud.

Penguins love the snow.

Farmers love to wake up early.
Roosters love to crow.

Zoe loves the library. Grover loves it, too.
Elmo whispers quietly, "Elmo loves *you*!"

The Count loves counting things.

Ernie loves to drum.

Monsters love to exercise.

Kids love bubble gum.

Natasha and her daddy love playing
    peekaboo.
But, *psssst!*—before you turn the
    page—Elmo loves *you*!

Monkeys love bananas.

Kids love school.

Grouches love trash.

Everyone loves something.
Elmo told you this was true.
And now you know who Elmo loves:
Elmo loves *you*!

Before he ends his poem, Elmo wants
   to ask you this:
Will you be Elmo's valentine?
Could Elmo have a kiss?